TALENT
FRIGHT

Steve Barlow and Steve Skidmore

Illustrated by Alex Lopez

LONDON·SYDNEY

Franklin Watts
First published in Great Britain in 2017 by The Watts Publishing Group

Credits
Executive Editor: Adrian Cole
Design Manager: Peter Scoulding
Cover Designer: Cathryn Gilbert
Illustrations: Alex Lopez

HB ISBN 978 1 4451 5253 0
PB ISBN 978 1 4451 5255 4
Library ebook ISBN 978 1 4451 5254 7

Printed in China.

MIX
Paper from
responsible sources
FSC® C104740
FSC
www.fsc.org

Franklin Watts
An imprint of
Hachette Children's Group
Part of The Watts Publishing Group
Carmelite House
50 Victoria Embankment
London EC4Y 0DZ

An Hachette UK Company
www.hachette.co.uk

www.franklinwatts.co.uk

Lin

Danny

Sam

"Nothing," said Lin. "Talent shows are boring."

"No they're not!" said Britney. "You don't have any talent. That's why you think they are boring."

"We have hidden talent!" said Danny.

"Yeah!" said Clogger. "Well hidden!"

"Wow!" said Danny.

Lin looked puzzled. "Were his fingers supposed to come off?"

"Did you see where they went?" wailed Sam. "Help me get them back!"

"We're useless," said Lin. "Britney was right — we don't have any talent!"

"Don't be too sure about that," said Danny. "Let's team up! We could do a hot magic show…"

"It's us next. What happens if they don't like us?" asked Lin.

Danny grinned. "Don't worry. We'll knock them dead!"

28